Charles Dickens

David Copperfield

塊肉餘生

Retold and With Activities by Alex Peet
Illustrated by Felicita sala

The Commercial Press

Contents 目錄

4 **Main Characters -** 人物介紹

6 **Before you read -** 讀前練習

8 Chapter 1 **"Mr Murdstone."**
悲劇開端
Activities

18 Chapter 2 **"School."**
寄人籬下
Activities

28 Chapter 3 **"Everything changes."**
孤身一人
Activities

38 Chapter 4 **"A new life."**
重獲新生
Activities

48 Chapter 5 **"Dora."**
美滿婚姻
Activities

58 Chapter 6 **"Endings and beginnings."**
是終是始？
Activities

70 Focus on... **Charles Dickens**
專題探索：作家查爾斯·狄更斯

72 Focus on... **Life in Victorian Times**
專題探索：英倫童工

74 Focus on... **CLIL - Education and Travel**
CLIL歷史學習：教育與交通

76 Test yourself - 自測

77 Syllabus - 語法重點和學習主題

78 Answer Key - 答案

David Copperfield

Dora Spenlow

Peggotty

Edward Murdstone

Miss Jane Murdstone

Clara Copperfield

Uriah Heep

Mr Micawber

Agnes Wickfield

Miss Betsey Trotwood

James Steerforth

Before you read

Vocabulary

1 **Match the words with their definitions.**

	f	nurse
1	☐	orphan
2	☐	step-father
3	☐	mourner
4	☐	niece
5	☐	nephew
6	☐	schoolmaster
7	☐	debtor
8	☐	clerk

a a person who works in an office.

b old word for teacher (male).

c your brother or sister's daughter.

d your mother's second husband.

e your brother or sister's son.

f a woman who looks after small children.

g a person attending a funeral.

h a person who is unable to pay money owed.

i a child whose parents are dead .

Speaking

2 **Look at the words above again. Use them to make predictions about what you think will happen in the story. Discuss with a partner.**

Grammar

3 **Complete this text about *David Copperfield* with the words in the box.**

> nurse   up   old   a   back   his   at   tells
> ~~and~~   as   the   to   a

Charles Dickens wrote *David Copperfield* between 1849
..........*and*.......... 1850. However it wasn't published (1) ....
a complete book at first: every month (2) .... few
chapters were published in a newspaper, so people had to
wait (3) .... discover what happened next, a bit like
people do now with their favourite soaps!
David Copperfield is (4) .... story of (5) ....
young boy. (6) .... the beginning of the story he is
eight years (7) .... and he lives happily with
(8) .... mother and (9) .... Unfortunately
David's life changes completely. In the book David looks
(10) .... on his life and (11) .... of his adventures
as a child and as he grew (12) ....

Vocabulary

4 **Read these descriptions of characters from the book and complete them with the following adjectives.**

> arrogant   kind-hearted   calm   formidable   severe

a He is intolerant and ....
b She is gentle and ....
c He is self-confident and a little ....
d She is austere and ....
e He is generous and ....

Chapter 1

Mr Murdstone

I disliked Mr Murdstone the first time I met him. Perhaps I was just jealous or perhaps it was more than that. Certainly he was a handsome gentleman with dark hair and dark whiskers[1] but there was something in his eyes that made me feel uneasy[2]. He began to call at our house and then my mother started putting on her prettiest dresses and going out in the evenings.

One such evening my nurse, Peggotty, suggested that I go with her to visit her brother in Yarmouth for a fortnight[3]. I agreed immediately, happy at the thought of an adventure. I did not realize how different things would be on my return.

The day of our departure soon arrived and Peggotty and I climbed into the carrier's cart[4] that was to take us to Yarmouth. My mother and I kissed each other and we both cried. When the cart started off she ran after it to ask for another kiss. As we rode away I saw Mr Murdstone speaking to her disapprovingly and she lowered her head submissively.

---

1. whiskers: 鬍鬚
2. uneasy: 不安
3. fortnight: 兩週 ▶PET◀
4. cart: 馬車

I shall never forget that holiday. Peggotty's nephew, Ham, was waiting for us when the cart set us down. He swung me on his broad[1] shoulders and took us to their home. The Peggottys lived in a boat that had been taken from the water and made into a small cosy[2] home. For a young boy like me it was magical. My nurse's brother, Mr Peggotty, greeted us warmly and introduced Little Emily, his niece. Both she and Ham were orphans. She was about my age with blue eyes and curls and I quickly became devoted to her. When it was time for me to leave we were both inconsolable.

As we approached home, however, I became excited about seeing my mother again. She was not at the gate to greet me and Peggotty led me into the kitchen. Now I was worried.

'Where is Mama, Peggotty? What has happened? She isn't dead, is she, like Papa?' Tears filled my eyes.

'Good gracious, no, Master Davy!' she replied shocked. 'But there is something I must tell you. You have a new pa! Come and see him. And your mama.'

We went into the best parlour[3]. My mother

---

1. **broad:** 寬闊
2. **cosy:** 舒適

3. **parlour:** 客廳 ▶SYN◀ living room

was sitting on one side of the fireplace and Mr Murdstone sat on the other side. As soon as she saw me, my mother smiled and hugged me timidly.

'Now, Clara, control yourself,' Mr Murdstone said. She kissed me avoiding looking at me under Mr Murdstone's watchful eye. As soon as I could, I went to my room. Miserable, I thought of how different things used to be, how loving and affectionate my mother had been under Peggotty's indulgent eye. I knew that happy life was over[1] and I cried myself to sleep.

I was awoken by my mother and Peggotty who had been looking for me.

'Davy, what is the matter?' my mother asked. She tried to put her arms around me but I pushed her away. 'Oh, this is your fault, Peggotty!' she cried. 'You have turned my boy against me!'

I heard other footsteps and Mr Murdstone entered. 'Clara, my dear, remember yourself!'

'Oh, it is too much!' my mother exclaimed. 'Can I not have some peace and happiness?' Mr Murdstone calmed her with a kiss and I saw immediately that she would do whatever he said.

'Go downstairs while David and I talk. We'll

---

1. **over:** 完結

join you shortly[1],' he said with a smile. When we were alone he asked me, 'Do you know what I do with a disobedient dog? I beat it.' He gave me a hard look and I understood all too well. 'Now, come downstairs and do not displease your mother or me again.'

After dinner that evening Mr Murdstone's sister arrived. She was dark like him, with the same stern[2] look, but had a large nose and thick eyebrows which almost met in the middle. She had come to help my mother, and started the next morning by rearranging all our store cupboards. From then on she took control of everything. On the one occasion that my mother asked to be consulted occasionally Mr Murdstone accused her of being ungrateful and expressed his disappointment. It was enough. My mother never protested again.

I resumed my lessons with my mother but these were no longer the happy times they had been before. Mr and Miss Murdstone were always present, always ready to criticize my mother for her lack[3] of firmness with me and myself for every mistake. Mr Murdstone made me nervous

---

1. **shortly:** 很快 ▶PET◀
2. **stern:** 嚴厲

3. **lack:** 缺乏

and forgetful. My mother in turn became anxious. When she thought no-one was looking she tried to help me but was immediately rebuked[1] by Miss Murdstone. My poor mother suffered as much as I did, if not more.

This continued for several months until one morning I entered the parlour for my lessons and saw my mother looking more nervous than usual. Mr Murdstone was holding a cane[2] in his hand.

'Now, David, you must be very careful over your lessons today,' he said. The effect was, of course, that I became particularly forgetful and things went from worse to worse. Finally my mother burst into tears.

'David, you and I will go upstairs,' Mr Murdstone said, taking my arm. My mother ran after us but Miss Murdstone stopped her. My mother's crying accompanied me up the stairs. When we got to my room Mr Murdstone suddenly pinned[3] my head under his arm and raised the cane in his other hand.

'Please, sir! Don't beat me! I'll do better!'

'Really?' he replied and hit me hard. The hand holding me was near my mouth and I bit it. He

---

1. rebuked: 斥責   3. pinned: 按住
2. cane: 藤條

beat me then again and again with renewed fury. I heard my mother and Peggotty crying outside the door and then it was over. He left me and locked the door behind him.

I was kept in my room for five days. The only person I saw was Miss Murdstone who brought me food but never spoke to me. On the fifth evening I heard whispering¹ at my door.

'Davy, my darling?' It was Peggotty.

'Oh, Peggotty!' I cried.

'Hush² or they will hear us, my lovely. Listen! You are going away to school tomorrow.'

1. **whispering:** 低語   2. **hush:** 噓 ▶SYN◀ be quiet

After-reading Activities

Reading

1 **Decide if the following statements are true (T) or false (F).**

		T	F
	David felt uncomfortable in Mr Murdstone's presence from the beginning.	☑	☐
1	The Peggottys lived on the water.	☐	☐
2	Peggotty knew about the marriage before David.	☐	☐
3	David realized his life had changed with his mother's marriage.	☐	☐
4	Miss Murdstone arrived on the same evening David returned home.	☐	☐
5	David's mother repeatedly asked to be consulted in domestic matters.	☐	☐
6	David's mother was afraid to openly help him with his lessons.	☐	☐
7	David bit Mr Murdstone's arm.	☐	☐

Vocabulary

2 **Form the opposites using the prefixes below.**

dis in ~~un~~ un dis

......*un*......grateful
1 ....approvingly   **3** ....please
2 ....consolable   **4** ....easy

3 **Find at least six words from the chapter to put in each column.**

Physical features/body	Personality
hair,	jealous,

16

Grammar

4 Write sentences using 'used to/didn't use to' and the prompts below.

1 David's mother / go out in the evenings.
2 Things / be different.
3 Mr Murdstone / live with them.
4 David's mother / be affectionate.
5 David / enjoy his lessons.

Before-reading Activities

Speaking

5 Discuss the following questions with a partner.

1 Do you think David will be happy at school Why (not)?
2 What will the school, teachers and other pupils be like?

Pet Listening

6 Listen to the description of the school and fill in the missing information.

Name: Salem **1** ....
Description: **2** .... building with a courtyard
Number of boys present on David's arrival: **3** ....
Description of classroom: dirty, long with rows of
4 ....
Sign saying: 'Be **5** .... He bites.'

Chapter 2

School

 I left after breakfast the following morning. My mother, her eyes red from crying, embraced me and told me to be good. Then Miss Murdstone took me to the awaiting cart.

It was the same carrier that had taken Peggotty and myself to Yarmouth. I cried heartily[1] as we drove away. Then, about half a mile from the house, Peggotty suddenly appeared from behind a hedge[2] and got into the cart. She hugged me tightly, put some cakes into my pockets, and got out again, all without saying a word. I felt a little happier after this and even more so when I found two half-crowns[3] wrapped in paper, sent with my mother's love.

As the morning progressed, I shared my cakes with the carrier and learnt that his name was Mr Barkis. He asked a few questions about Peggotty and then asked me to give her a message when I wrote to her.

'What message is that, Mr Barkis?' I asked.

---

1. **heartily:** 盡情
2. **hedge:** 樹籬
3. **half-crowns:** 舊日英國錢幣，約等於現時12便士

'Tell her: Barkis is willing[1]', he replied. I thought it a strange message but kept the thought to myself. I very soon fell asleep.

Mr Barkis set me down at the inn in Yarmouth where, after some dinner, I took the stagecoach[2] to London. We travelled through the night and I sat pressed in between two gentlemen. Unlike the other passengers I was unable to sleep.

We arrived in London the next morning. Nobody was waiting for me at the inn so the coachman left me in the booking office. I began to think I might never be claimed and that perhaps this was Mr Murdstone's revenge, when a thin young man entered. His name was Mr Mell and he was a schoolmaster at my new school.

Salem House was an unwelcoming, square brick building. As we crossed the courtyard I remarked to Mr Mell how quiet it was. He seemed surprised.

'Copperfield, don't you know it is the school holidays? There are no boys here, except you.'

Mr Mell left me in the classroom for a while. It

---

1. **willing:** 樂意 ▶PET◀   2. **stagecoach:** 驛馬車

was a soulless, dirty, long, room which smelt stale[1] and unhealthy. I walked up and down the rows[2] of desks, noticing the scraps of paper on the floor and the ink splashed liberally about.

At one end of the room I saw a beautifully written sign lying on a desk. It said "Be careful. He bites."

I imagined it was for a fierce dog and felt rather alarmed. So I quickly climbed up onto the neighbouring desk and proceeded to peer[3] under the other desks in search of it. When Mr Mell returned he found me like this and asked what I was doing.

'I'm looking for the dog, sir,' I replied. He looked at me gravely[4].

'I'm sorry, Copperfield,' he said, 'it's for you. I've been instructed to make you wear it.' He helped me down from the desk and put the sign over my head so that it hung on my back. How mortified I was! How I suffered! I was glad there was nobody there to see it.

As the days and weeks passed I began to dread[5] the end of the holidays but it was inevitable. Preparations were made for the boys' return and one

1. **stale:** 不新鮮
2. **rows:** 行
3. **peer:** 仔細看
4. **gravely:** 嚴肅地
5. **dread:** 擔憂

morning it was announced that the headmaster, Mr Creakle, would return that evening. After supper I was summoned[1] before him.

Mr Creakle, who was almost completely bald, had an angry face with small eyes and nose and a large chin. He never spoke above a whisper and, judging by the veins protruding[2] on his forehead, the effort cost him dearly.

'I know your step-father, boy,' he said, as I stood before him. 'And I know something about you: you bite.' I lowered my head and he continued. 'Let me tell you something about myself. I'm a Tartar and very determined. I do my duty and make sure what I want done is done. Nobody stands in my way. Do I make myself clear?'

'Yes, sir,' I replied, trembling under his fiery gaze[3].

'Good. Now go,' he replied. I hurried away as quickly as possible.

The first boy I met was Tommy Traddles. He found the sign on my back so amusing that he immediately introduced me to all the other boys as they arrived back. However, the most important

1. **summoned:** 傳喚
2. **protruding:** 凸出

3. **gaze:** 凝視

introduction took place in the playground and was to a boy some six years older than myself, who was respected and admired by all the boys in the school.

Steerforth, for this was his name, asked me why I had to wear the sign and, hearing my story, declared it was a shame[1]. I became devoted to him immediately and he took me under his wing.

School was a sorry business. Mr Creakle was indeed a Tartar and took great delight in using his cane. He seemed to particularly enjoy caning the chubbier[2] boys and a day never passed without poor Traddles receiving a beating. The only exception was Steerforth who Mr Creakle never raised his cane to.

The months passed and finally the holidays came and I went home. I was so excited to see my mother and Peggotty. My mother was sitting in the parlour when I arrived, with a baby in her arms. She looked thinner and more fragile than before, although still pretty. On seeing me she got up to embrace me.

1. **shame:** 恥辱　　　　　2. **chubbier:** 較胖的

'Davy, my boy! I'm so happy to see you! This is your little brother,' she said showing me the baby.

Peggotty came running in then and held me to her.

'Oh, Master Davy! Let me look at you!'

That evening was the best day of the holiday. Mr and Miss Murdstone were not at home and we three all dined together. I told them about Mr Creakle and Steerforth and we talked and laughed. I almost believed Mr Murdstone did not exist until we heard the door open later on. My mother suggested I went to bed quickly: Mr Murdstone did not approve of going to bed late. I said goodnight and slipped[1] out of the room.

The next morning Mr Murdstone was sitting in the parlour. I approached fearfully and apologised for biting him. He accepted my apology coldly but nothing changed between us. The rest of the holidays were quite miserable. Whenever I entered the room in the middle of a conversation, Mr Murdstone or his sister stopped speaking and became serious while my mother looked anxiously from one to the other. I, therefore, tried to remain out of the way and sat silently through meals. This behaviour drew[2]

---

1. **slipped:** 溜走   2. **drew:** 引起

criticism too and if my mother attempted weakly to defend me she was also rebuked.

Finally the day came to return to school. My mother came to the gate to say goodbye. When I was sitting in the cart, she held up the baby for me to see and stood that way as we drove away. I did not know it but this would be my last image of her.

Now I must relate the saddest time of my life. My birthday was about two months after my return to school. After breakfast, I was told to go to the parlour. I imagined that Peggotty or my mother had sent something for me but was conscious of something like pity in the schoolmaster's eyes.

Mr Creakle was still at the breakfast table when I arrived but he quickly left the room. His wife sat me down beside her and, with a sad look, took my hand.

'My poor boy, sit beside me. I'm afraid I have some very sad news: your mother has died.'

I cried long and hard while Mrs Creakle held me. The news quickly spread[1] through the school and I had the bitter[2] satisfaction of a new-found status among the boys.

---

1. **spread:** 傳開   2. **bitter:** 痛苦 ▶PET◀

Pet Reading

1 **Read the summary and complete the spaces. For each space choose A, B, C, or D.**

Example: **A** a   **B** the   **C** an   **D** such

Answer:

0	A	B	C	D
	☐	☐	▬	☐

Salem House was (0) ....*C*............ unwelcoming place. When David arrived there weren't (1) .... boys there apart (2) .... him. Mr Mell left him in the classroom (3) .... was soulless and dirty. There he found a sign (4) .... on a desk: it said 'Be careful. He bites.' David thought the sign was for a dog but Mr Mell told him it was for him and he (5) .... to wear it at all (6) ....

That evening he met Mr Creakle who was an angry little man who spoke in a whisper. He told David that he always (7) .... his duty and made sure everything he wanted was done. David was frightened of him and left the room as (8) .... as possible when told to. David was not happy at school (9) .... Mr Creakles was a cruel man who beat the boys regularly. (10) .... this he made some friends, in particular Steerforth.

1	**A** any	**B** no	**C** none	**D** lots
2	**A** of	**B** for	**C** from	**D** to
3	**A** which	**B** what	**C** where	**D** when
4	**A** lie	**B** lying	**C** lies	**D** lay
5	**A** should	**B** would	**C** must	**D** had
6	**A** time	**B** ages	**C** times	**D** hour
7	**A** made	**B** carried	**C** did	**D** had
8	**A** quick	**B** quickly	**C** quicker	**D** quickest
9	**A** because	**B** but	**C** so	**D** or
10	**A** Part	**B** Except	**C** But	**D** Despite

Grammar

2 **Complete these sentences using the past simple or past continuous.**

David ....*shared*........ his cakes with Mr Barkis while they ....*went*........ to Yarmouth *(share, go)*.

1 Nobody .... for David when the stagecoach .... in London *(wait, arrive)*.

2 When Mr Mell .... he .... David standing on a desk *(return, find)*.

3 David's mother .... in the parlour when he .... *(sit, enter)*.

4 She .... up to embrace him as soon as she .... him *(get, see)*.

5 While Mr Murdstone and his sister .... out for the evening, David, his mother and Peggotty all .... together *(be, dine)*.

6 Mr Creakle .... his breakfast when David .... into the parlour *(have, go)*.

Pre-reading Activity

Reading

3 **What do you think happens next? Decide if these sentences are true (T) or false (F). Then read the next chapter and check.**

	T	F
1 Mr Murdstone treats David more kindly.	☐	☐
2 David's baby brother dies too.	☐	☐
3 Peggotty gets married.	☐	☐
4 David is sent to work.	☐	☐

Chapter 3

Everything changes

 And so the worst period of my life began. I was sent home the next day but any hope I had of finding much comfort there was immediately dashed[1]. Mr Murdstone ignored my presence entirely and sat consumed by his own grief[2] while his sister busied herself with practical matters. I saw little of Peggotty except at night when she sat by my bed and offered me the only comfort I found under that roof.

The time before the funeral is confused in my memory but I remember the day itself clearly. I can still see the best parlour readied for mourners and later the coffin[3] containing my mother and baby brother as it was lowered into the ground.

That evening Peggotty came to my room. She held me close and told me that my mother had died in her arms, her last thoughts of me. The baby had died the following day.

The first thing Miss Murdstone did after the funeral was over, was to give Peggotty a month's

1. dashed: 擊碎
2. grief: 哀痛

3. coffin: 棺材

28

notice[1]. Poor Peggotty was as upset as I was at the thought of our separation.

After her departure I was almost entirely neglected. I ate with the Murdstones when they were at home, alone when they were not. Mr Murdstone tried to see as little of me as possible, my presence, perhaps, irritating his conscience, and I spent many lonely hours, weeks, months. Peggotty, now married to Mr Barkis, came to visit as often as she was allowed but it was never often enough. Then, one day, Mr Murdstone decided I should be sent to work in his business in London. I was ten years old.

Murdstone and Grinby's warehouse[2] was in Black-friars[3], on the waterfront. It was an old building, overrun[4] with rats. My job, along with four other boys was to wash, label and pack the bottles of wine the warehouse shipped overseas. For this I received six shillings[5] a week. Lodgings were arranged for me with Mr Micawber, who I was introduced to on my first day. He was a rotund middle-aged man

---

1. **notice:** 離職通知 ▶PET◀
2. **warehouse:** 貨倉
3. **Blackfriars:** 黑衣修士區
4. **overrun:** 滿佈
5. **shillings:** 先令

with a shiny bald head. His clothes were shabby[1] yet he had an air of kindness. Mr Micawber lived with his wife and four children in a house which was as shabby as he was.

I worked from morning to night and spent all my earnings on my breakfast and supper, which was often an inadequate affair. I was quite miserable at work, feeling the full shame[2] of my situation and the divide between myself and the other men and boys there. I had no friends, so I became attached to the Micawber family. Mrs Micawber freely confided all of her husband's financial problems to me and enlisted my services in selling household possessions. Thus I bore[3] not only my own misery but also my worries for this kind family.

Finally Mr Micawber's problems reached a crisis. Unable to repay his creditors, he was arrested and taken to a debtors' prison. Soon afterwards the family furniture was sold and Mrs Micawber and the children moved into his cell[4] with him. I did not want to be separated from the only family I knew in London so lodgings were found for me near the prison.

1. **shabby:** 殘舊的
2. **shame:** 羞愧 ▶PET◀
3. **bore:** 忍受
4. **cell:** 囚室

After several weeks Mr Micawber was released from prison and we were all reunited. However, he decided to leave London and wasted very little time in preparations. We spent their last evening together and Mr Micawber offered me some fatherly advice.

'My dear Copperfield,' he said, 'learn from my mistakes. Never put off[1] until tomorrow what you can do today.' I promised not to.

After my friends left I felt I could bear it no longer at Murdstone and Grinby's and a plan formed in my mind. I would run away. I remembered my mother telling me about my father's aunt, Betsey Trotswood. Disappointed[2] that I was a boy and not a girl, she had severed all ties[3] with my mother at my birth. Despite this, I decided to find her and ask for her help.

I shall not relate my journey: how I was robbed almost immediately of my possessions, how I walked all day and slept in fields at night, selling my jacket and waistcoat in order to buy food. It is enough to say that six days after I left London I arrived, exhausted, starving[4] and half-clothed in Dover and began to enquire after my aunt.

---

1. **put off:** 拖延
2. **disappointed:** 失望 ▶PET◀
3. **severed all ties:** 斷絕聯絡
4. **starving:** 非常飢餓

I was lucky and after no more than half a day I was following her maid[1] along a cliff[2] road to the pretty cottage in which my aunt lived. There, aware of my terrible appearance, my courage failed. Having stood outside for a while I was intending to leave when an elderly lady came out of the cottage. She was wearing gardening gloves and a handkerchief over her bonnet[3] and held a large knife in her hand.

'Go away! I'll have no boys here!' she said angrily before turning away. I approached and, timidly touching her, said, 'Please, ma'am[4]. I'm your nephew, David Copperfield.'

'Good gracious!' she exclaimed, sitting down quickly. A series of emotions passed across her face. I hurriedly[5] told her all my story and then burst into tears. Seeing this she took me by the collar, led me into the cottage and lay me on the sofa. She then instructed her maid, Janet, to ask Mr Dick to come downstairs. Soon afterwards a grey-haired gentleman appeared.

'Mr Dick, do you remember my nephew David Copperfield?' she asked him.

1. maid: 女傭
2. cliff: 懸崖 ▶PET◀
3. bonnet: 女裝帽
4. ma'am: 女士
5. hurriedly: 趕快

'Well, this is his son and he's run away. What should we do?'

Mr Dick considered for a moment and then said 'Give him a bath.' And so I was bathed, fed and, much restored, put to bed.

The following morning I entered the parlour feeling quite hopeful. My aunt was an austere woman but not unkind. Perhaps she would let me stay with her.

'Good morning, David,' she said. 'I have written to your step-father and told him to come.'

'Oh, must I go back?' I asked, my voice failing.

'I haven't decided. We shall see,' she replied. My hopes died.

On the morning Mr Murdstone came, we were sitting in the parlour. Aunt Betsey suddenly saw a lady on a donkey approach the house. My aunt never allowed donkeys on the grass and angrily shook[1] her fist[2] at the rider from the window. Recognising Miss Murdstone, I quickly informed my aunt of the rider's identity.

'I don't care!' she cried and ran outside, shaking her fist again. Mr Murdstone was walking up behind

---

1. **shook:** 搖動   2. **fist:** 拳頭

his sister. They both looked at my aunt in surprise.

She ignored them and chased away[1] the boy leading the donkey. Then she marched back into the house and waited for Janet to announce the visitors.

'Miss Trotswood,' said Mr Murdstone on entering, 'I have come to take this ungrateful boy back.'

'Really? David, are you ready to leave?' my aunt asked me.

'No! They never liked me and made Mama unhappy about me too! Please don't send me back with them! I was so miserable!' I exclaimed.

'This is ridiculous!' said Miss Murdstone indignantly.

'I wonder[2], would you treat your own son like this and send him to work?' my aunt asked Mr Murdstone.

'I can do what I like with the boy. I must warn you, Miss Trotswood, if you decide to keep him I shall close my door to him forever,' Mr Murdstone said sternly.

'So be it! I shall take my chances with him. Good day to you both,' my aunt replied coldly. 'Janet, show them out!' Furious, the Murdstones marched out of the house and out of my life.

1. **chased away:** 趕走   2. **wonder:** 想知道 ▶PET◀

After-reading Activities

Reading

1 Answer these questions.

  1 What did David think might be Mr Murdstone's reason for seeing as little of him as possible?

  ....

  2 Where was Mr Murdstone's warehouse situated?

  ....

  3 How much did David earn?

  ....

  4 What sort of problems did Mr Micawber have?

  ....

Vocabulary

2 Replace the underlined words or phrases in the sentences below with words or phrases from the box.

> accommodation was   asked for my help
> total humiliation   not looked after
> sent it abroad by ship   started crying

  After Peggotty's departure I was <u>neglected</u>.
  ..not looked after..

1 Murdstone and Grinby's bottled wine and <u>shipped it overseas</u>. ....

2 <u>Lodgings were</u> arranged for me with Mr Micawber.

  ....

3 I felt the <u>full shame</u> of my situation. ....

4 Mrs Micawber <u>enlisted my services</u> in selling household possessions. ....

5 I told my aunt my story and then <u>burst into tears</u>.

  ....

3 Here are some sentences about the story in this chapter. For each question, complete the second sentence so that it means the same as the first. Use no more than three words. Only write the missing words.

As soon as the funeral was over, Miss Murdstone gave Peggotty her notice.

After the funeral, Miss Murdstone ..*immediately*.. *gave Peggotty her notice.*

1 David worked with four other boys.

.... four other boys who worked with David.

2 David spent all his earnings on his breakfast and supper.

David used all his earnings .... for his breakfast and supper.

3 The police arrested Mr Micawber for debt.

Mr Micawber .... the police for debt.

4 'Do you remember my nephew, David Copperfield?' Aunt Betsey asked him.

Aunt Betsey asked him .... her nephew, David Copperfield.

5 Aunt Betsey was much kinder than Mr Murdstone.

Mr Murdstone wasn't nearly .... Aunt Betsey.

Before-reading Activity

Listening

4 Decide if the following statements about the next chapter are true (T) or false (F).

                                                            T F

1 David is not happy with his aunt.   ☐ ☐
2 Aunt Betsey calls David by a different name.   ☐ ☐
3 Aunt Betsey decides to send David away to school.   ☐ ☐
4 David runs away.   ☐ ☐
5 David meets a nice girl.   ☐ ☐

Chapter 4

A new life

 My life now took a happy turn. I became good friends with Mr Dick and my aunt, who called me Trot, grew very fond of me. She decided to seek the advice of a certain Mr Wickfield, her lawyer, regarding a suitable school for me in Canterbury. I accompanied her to his house. When we arrived a pale[1] youth[2] of about fifteen opened the door to us. He had extremely short red hair, no eyebrows or eyelashes and was bony and ill-proportioned with skeleton-like hands. His name was Uriah Heep.

'Uriah, is Mr Wickfield at home?' my aunt asked. He showed us into the study. Mr Wickfield soon arrived. He was an affable[3] gentleman with white hair and a complexion which suggested a little too much port[4]. He was able not only to recommend a school but to offer me lodgings in his house. Then he introduced me to his daughter, Agnes. She was about my age with a gentle face and such a calm spirit that I have never forgotten. I knew immediately that we would be friends.

1. **pale:** 蒼白 ▶PET◀
2. **youth:** 青年 ▶PET◀
3. **affable:** 和善
4. **port:** 波爾多葡萄酒

So time passed. I attended Doctor Strong's school. It would be impossible to find someone more different from Mr Creakle: Doctor Strong was one of the kindest, gentlest men I have ever known and my schooldays there were happy ones. I was also happy living in Mr Wickfield's house and grew close to Agnes, coming to consider her as a sister. The only person I did not like there was Uriah Heep. I had disliked him instinctively on first meeting him and the years did nothing to change this. He continually referred to himself as 'a humble person' and had snakelike movements and ingratiating[1] ways which repulsed me.

Finally the time came for me to leave school and take my place in the world. I was seventeen. At my aunt's suggestion I took some time to think about what I wanted to do next, and decided to visit my dear old nurse, Peggotty. I took the stagecoach to London, stopping for the night at an inn there. As I sat near the fire, a handsome, well-dressed, young man entered the room. It was Steerforth!

'Steerforth! Don't you recognise me?' I asked, approaching him, hand outstretched. He looked at

---

1. **ingratiating:** 奉承的

me hard and then I saw recognition light up his face.

'Why it is Copperfield!' he exclaimed, shaking my hand heartily.

'I'm so glad to see you!' I said, tears coming to my eyes. We sat and talked. He was on his way from Oxford University to see his mother and suggested I went with him. I agreed happily and we set off[1] the next morning.

I spent a delightful week with them during which Steerforth taught me to ride. When I finally made up my mind to continue my journey, Steerforth decided to accompany me. And so we travelled to Yarmouth together. When Peggotty recognised me, joy spread across her face and we fell into each other's arms.

Steerforth charmed Peggotty with his easy ways and affection for me. That evening we all went to Mr Peggotty's little boat and knocked on the door. We could hear the sound of laughing and celebrating coming from inside.

'Look who is with me, brother?' Peggotty said, indicating myself.

1. set off: 起程

'Why, Master Copperfield!' Mr Peggotty exclaimed, shaking my hand and then Steerforth's.

'What are you celebrating, if I might ask?' I enquired, looking round the room at everyone.

'Such good news! My Emily is to marry Ham!' Mr Peggotty said happily taking Emily's hand in his. She blushed prettily. What a beauty she had become! Ham stood grinning[1] with pride.

'Well! Congratulations!' I said, shaking his hand and smiling at Emily.

We spent a happy evening. Steerforth entertained everyone with stories of the sea. Emily sat in a corner but observed and listened to everything. When we left her blue eyes followed Steerforth.

We remained in Yarmouth for a fortnight although not always together. I enjoyed wandering[2] on my own and went to visit my childhood home. Sadly I found the windows closed up and the garden overgrown[3]. Steerforth spent a great deal of time with Mr Peggotty, sailing. At last a letter arrived from my aunt, reminding me of my purpose[4] and inviting me to join her in London.

---

1. grinning: 露齒而笑
2. wandering: 閒逛
3. overgrown: 雜草叢生
4. purpose: 目的 ▶PET◀

It was decided: I would become a proctor[1]. My aunt found me a position as a clerk with Spenlow & Jorkins and we found lodgings nearby. Imagine my delight when I met Traddles again in London, lodging with my old friend Mr Micawber!

After a trial period I was articled[2]. Mr Spenlow invited me to his house, Norwood, for the weekend. When we arrived, he immediately called for his daughter. We entered a room and there she was. Dora Spenlow! I fell in love instantly.

Later we walked in the garden together. She wore a straw hat and, had such blue eyes and curls! A little black dog, Jip, was by her side. We made idle[3] conversation and walked together to the greenhouse. There, she stopped to admire the geraniums and, laughing charmingly, held Jip in her arms. I followed her from flower to flower, her slave.

Dora became my life. I thought of her constantly and walked along the road to Norwood so many times hoping to see her that I soon became well-known there.

1. **proctor:** 律師
2. **articled:** 當見習律師
3. **idle:** 輕鬆

I saw Steerforth occasionally when he came up to London. On one such occasion he brought me news from Yarmouth. Mr Barkis, Peggotty's husband, was dying. I resolved to go to Peggotty and obtained permission from Mr Spenlow.

In the days following Mr Barkis's death I helped settle[1] his affairs for Peggotty and then stayed for the funeral. That evening we were all to meet at Mr Peggotty's house but Ham and Emily did not arrive. After a while I went outside and saw Ham there, his head in his hands.

'Ham, what is the matter?' I asked. He looked at me with dead eyes.

'How can I tell him, Master Davy? How can I tell him that Emily has run away?' he exclaimed.

'Run away? Where to? Who with?' I asked. I looked at Ham's face and knew. Steerforth.

You may well imagine the misery that I witnessed that evening and the feeling of loss greater than death that fell upon the house. Mr Peggotty resolved to find Emily and never rest until he did.

1. **settle:** 處理妥當

My sadness at the Peggotty's troubles weighed heavily upon me and was lightened only by an invitation to Dora's birthday party. It was a picnic in the countryside. A young man with red whiskers claimed Dora's attention and, in a state of jealousy, I flirted[1] with the nearest girl I could find. I was miserable all afternoon. I was planning to leave when Dora approached with a friend.

'Mr Copperfield you are unhappy. Dora so are you,' the wise[2] friend said. 'Stop this silliness now before it is too late.' Without thinking I took Dora's hand and kissed it and she let me. I offered her my arm and we walked together, I do not know where. What joy!

The next day I determined to declare myself. Alone with Dora I told her how happy I had been with her the day before. When she doubted it I took her in my arms and told her that I worshipped her. Jip barked[3] and growled[4] but I did not stop. I told her I could not live without her. She cried and I held her more tightly. Soon we were engaged.

---

1. **flirted:** 調情
2. **wise:** 明智 ▸PET◂

3. **barked:** 吠
4. **growled:** 低聲咆哮

Reading

1 **Number these events 1 – 9 according to the order in which they happened.**

A ☐ Mr Barkis died.

B ☐ David fell in love with Dora Spenlow.

C ☐ Emily and Ham decided to get married.

D ☐ David went to school in Canterbury.

E ☐ Emily ran away with Steerforth.

F ☐ David met Agnes Wickfield.

G ☐ David saw Steerforth again after several years.

H ☐ Dora had a birthday party.

I ☐ David was given a job as a clerk.

2 **Match the names of the people with the explanation of who they are.**

1 ☐ Mr Strong
2 ☐ Mr Wickfield
3 ☐ Uriah Heep
4 ☐ Agnes
5 ☐ Mr Spenlow
6 ☐ Dora

a Aunt Betsey's lawyer.
b Mr Spenlow's daughter and the girl David loves.
c David's teacher.
d David's employer.
e Mr Wickfield's daughter and David's friend.
f A youth who works for Mr Wickfield.

Grammar

3 **Use the past simple of the verbs in the box to complete the sentences below.**

| grow   fall   find   see   know   teach   ~~become~~   spend |

David ......*became*...... good friends with Mr Dick.

1 His aunt .... fond of him.

2 When David met Agnes he .... they would be good friends.

3 David .... recognition in Steerforth's face.

4 David .... a week at Steerforth's house and Steerforth .... him to ride.

5 David .... the windows of his childhood home closed and the garden overgrown.

6 David .... in love with Dora.

Pet Speaking

4 **Talk with a partner about the sort of jobs you would like to have in the future and why. Then talk about the sort of jobs you wouldn't like to have.**

Before-reading Activity

Vocabulary

5 **Match the words with their definitions.**

1 ☐ carefree
2 ☐ unwilling
3 ☐ pet name
4 ☐ toast
5 ☐ troubled

a an affectionate name
b happy and without worries
c worried
d not wanting to
e a tribute to someone made with raised wineglasses

Chapter 5

Dora

 Apart from Agnes, to whom I wrote immediately, and Dora's wise friend, Miss Mills, who she was staying with, we told no-one of our engagement. We met when we could and exchanged letters daily. We were so happy and in love!

However, this carefree existence did not last long. A series of events tested our love. The first was the discovery that my aunt was ruined. I found her, and Mr Dick, sitting outside my rooms one day. This news was a terrible shock and I confess my thoughts were not only for my aunt. I was poor now too and not the same man Dora had given her heart to.

My aunt stayed with me and we found accommodation for Mr Dick. I immediately spoke to Mr Spenlow about my circumstances but he was unwilling to release me from my articles. Consequently I determined to find additional work to support myself. I was lucky. My old teacher, Mr Strong, needed a secretary and we arranged that I should work for him for a couple of hours in the mornings and evenings.

The following Sunday I went to confess everything to Dora.

'My darling, could you love a poor man?' I asked, kissing her hand.

'Don't be so silly[1], Doady,' she replied, calling me by her pet name for me. 'I shall make Jip bite you if you don't stop!' When she realized I was serious she began to cry. I comforted her and promised to work hard and make everything right.

'Don't talk about hard work,' she said. She was terrified by the idea and more so when I suggested she learn something of how to keep house and cook. She trembled and cried. I resolved not to worry Dora again with such matters.

The second and third events came together. Mr Spenlow discovered our relationship and threatened[2] to change his will[3] if I refused to give Dora up. He gave me a week to consider. That same night he set out for home but died on the way. Dora was distraught[4] at her father's death and refused to

---

1. silly: 愚蠢 ▶PET◀
2. threatened: 威脅
3. will: 遺囑
4. distraught: 心煩意亂

see me. In fact there was no will, but there were debts and Dora was sent to live with two old aunts.

I was very depressed by my separation from Dora and, seeing me in this state, my aunt sent me to Dover to check on her cottage and its new tenant[1]. I stopped in Canterbury on the way back to visit Agnes. Mr Micawber was now working for Heep. He opened the door to me. We talked for a while before Agnes arrived. I confided all my problems to her and felt peace in doing so. She was always so kind and tender. She advised writing to Dora's aunts, telling them everything and asking for permission to visit from time to time. I immediately saw the wisdom of her words and resolved to write that day.

Uriah and his mother now lived in the house and so were present at dinner. I was conscious of them both watching Agnes and me throughout the evening. They seemed like a pair of evil[2] bats to me. The mother was constantly present the next day too until, unable to bear her presence any longer, I went for a walk to escape. I soon heard footsteps behind me. It was Uriah.

1. tenant: 租客   2. evil: 邪惡

'Why do you and your mother keep watching Miss Wickfield and I?' I asked him.

'You are a dangerous rival, Mr Copperfield,' he replied.

'Rival? Do you think I consider Miss Wickfield other than a sister?'

'Perhaps, perhaps not,' he said, 'but you must know, I hope to make her mine one day.'

'She is as far above you as the moon,' I said with feeling. He smiled slyly[1].

That evening after dinner Mr Wickfield, Uriah and I were alone. Uriah encouraged Mr Wickfield to drink and proposed a toast to Agnes.

'Ah, Mr Wickfield, to be her husband....' I heard a terrible cry from Mr Wickfield.

'Oh, this is torture!' he exclaimed. 'Is it not enough that I have let him into my business and my house? That I have lost my good name and reputation? No, he wants my daughter too! It is too much.'

'Be careful what you say! Remember I know things, Mr Wickfield,' Uriah said menacingly[2]. Agnes arrived then.

1. slyly: 狡猾地   2. menacingly: 威嚇地

'Papa, what is wrong?' she asked. 'Come, let me help you to bed,' she said, then looked at myself and Uriah.

I left Uriah there too and went upstairs. I was greatly troubled by what I had seen. Agnes came to me later. Her eyes were red from crying but she smiled.

'Agnes, promise me you will not think of sacrificing yourself to Uriah.' She smiled sadly and left me. I left the next morning full of concern.

The letter I wrote to Dora's aunts on Agnes's advice bore fruit[1]. I was invited to call. The aunts had considered my letter carefully and would allow me to visit every Sunday and twice during the week. I agreed immediately. Dora came in then. How happy I was to see her and how she cried!

Let me turn my recollections to a later date. I am twenty-one and Dora and I are married. Among my other occupations I have begun writing and Dora is never happier than when she sits next to me in the evenings, a supply[2] of pens in her hand. She feels

---

1. **bore fruit:** 取得成果   2. **supply:** 一把（量詞）

she is helping me and I indulge her, loving to see her so happy. I remember it all so well!

We had a little house in Highgate but Dora proved incapable of mastering accounts or cookery. One evening after a disastrous dinner she sat on my knee with her arms wrapped[1] around my neck.

'Doady, I'm so sorry. Will you do something for me? Will you think of me as your 'child-wife'? Then, when I do something wrong, perhaps you will forgive me more easily,' she said, earnestly.

'My child-wife,' I said, holding her close. I was rewarded[2] by her beautiful laugh. I never forgot this heartfelt appeal[3] and, although I sometimes wished she were more practical, I learned to accept her as she was and always loved her dearly.

In our second year of marriage Dora fell ill. We thought she would soon be her old self again but it was not to be. She spent more and more time resting on the sofa during the day and I carried her tenderly to bed in the evenings.

News came of Emily. She had been found! Mr Peggotty thought it would be best for her to start a new life far away and decided to emigrate with

---

1. **wrapped:** 環繞   3. **appeal:** 請求
2. **rewarded:** 獎賞

her to Australia. He asked me to accompany him to Yarmouth to tell everyone and, leaving Dora in my aunt's care, I agreed. I did not feel I should be present when he told Ham so I left him to break the news. Later I saw Ham standing alone looking out to sea. We talked briefly but never directly about Emily. Feeling he wanted to ask me something I went to look for him the next day.

'May I ask you something, Master Copperfield? Should I see her before she leaves?' he asked me.

'No, I don't think so. I think it would be too hard for her,' I replied. 'If you want to tell her something, I could write a letter for you, Ham,' I offered.

'Thank you. You are a gentleman and so much better with words than I am. I don't think I can forgive her or forget her but I don't want to weigh heavy on her heart. Tell her that I'm fine. Not that I shall ever marry or anything, but I'm fine,' he said. Poor, honest Ham! I promised to write for him.

Mr Peggotty emptied his little home the next day and packed the few things he wanted to take away and we travelled back to London together.

Reading

1 Write questions for these answers.

1 ....?

Only Agnes and Dora's friend, Miss Mills.

2 ....?

Three events.

3 ....?

Because her father died and there were debts.

4 ....?

He was horrified and thought it was torture.

5 ....?

He was twenty-one.

6 ....?

Because it was best for Emily to have a new start.

Grammar

2 Complete these sentences with the first or second conditional.

'If you ......*don't stop*...... talking I ......*will make*........ you. *(not stop, make)*

1 'We .... you so closely if we .... you a rival.' *(not watch, not consider)*

2 'I .... my will unless you .... up Dora'. *(change, give)*

3 'If I .... poor, I .... to work so hard,' David said. *(not be, not need)*

4 'If you .... of me as a child-wife, perhaps you .... me more easily when I do something wrong.' *(think, forgive)*

Pet writing

3 You are Dora. This is part of a letter you receive from a friend.

I heard you got married recently. Congratulations. What was the wedding like? Are you enjoying married life? Write and tell me.

Write a letter to your friend telling her about the wedding and your life with David.

Writing

4 Choose the correct form.

David and Dora were *so/such* happy and in love!

1 Aunt Betsey's news was *such a/so* shock for David.

2 'Don't be *so a/so* silly, Doady.'

3 Agnes and David were *such a/such* good friends.

4 David remembered everything *so/such* well.

Before-reading Activity

Listening

5 Listen and answer these questions.

1 What did David receive from Mr Micawber?

2 Who did Mr Micawber want to meet?

3 How was Mr Micawber when they met him?

4 Who did David want to introduce Mr Micawber to?

5 Where did Mr Micawber want everyone to go?

Chapter 6

Endings and beginnings

 I shall now relate how Uriah Heep was exposed for the villain[1] he was but, to do so, I must first go back a little in time. Shortly before Emily was found I received a mysterious letter from Mr Micawber: he was coming to London and wished to meet with me and Traddles. We waited for him at the appointed[2] time and found him to be quite agitated. Wanting to get to the bottom of things, I invited him to come to Highgate with me, where I would introduce him to my aunt. He accepted.

My aunt and Mr Dick welcomed him warmly. He was moved[3] by their hospitality but was clearly upset[4] about something.

'Mr Micawber, you are among friends here. Won't you tell us what is wrong?' I asked him.

'What is wrong? Heep, that is what is wrong! He is a villain! When I think of poor Miss Wickfield, so good, so loving and her poor father.....' Here he became extremely agitated. 'I shall not rest until I have exposed him. You must all come to Canterbury

1. **villain:** 壞人
2. **appointed:** 指定
3. **moved:** 被感動
4. **upset:** 煩擾 ▶PET◀

- one week from now.' He left us then abruptly, too upset to continue.

The next day a letter arrived repeating his request and giving us instructions. When the time came, my aunt and I were reluctant to leave Dora but she coaxed[1] us prettily, saying she was not so very ill. Not wanting to alarm her with our concerns for her health, we agreed to go.

So, as instructed, we went to Canterbury and called at the agreed time to see Agnes. Mr Micawber opened the door to us, pretending[2] to be surprised. Uriah certainly was. Agnes soon arrived. Uriah then instructed Mr Micawber to leave on some business but my old friend refused. Irritated, Uriah called him a scoundrel[3] and threatened to dismiss him but still Mr Micawber stayed.

'The only scoundrel here is you, I Iccp!' Micawber declared. Uriah looked at us all, surprised and then suspicious.

'Ah, this is a conspiracy, is it? Well, Copperfield you always were jealous of my rise. Miss Wickfield, if you love your father, do not join in this plot[4]. Miss

1. coaxed: 哄騙
2. pretending: 假裝
3. scoundrel: 惡棍
4. plot: 陰謀

Trotwood too, if you know what is best for you,' Uriah said, dropping all pretence of humility.

The change in him was astonishing. With his mask off, all his hatred and malice were apparent. He seemed to grow in height like an evil genie and I readily imagined him towering over poor Agnes and her father, frightening them into submission. Or, as he had threatened, turning his attention to my aunt. He was dangerous like a cornered[1] wild animal.

Unafraid, Mr Micawber took a burnt pocket-book[2] from his pocket.

'My wife found this in the fire when we moved into your house, Heep. Do you recognise it?' Uriah tried to snatch it but Mr Micawber was too quick. Addressing us he explained, 'It contains proof of fraud[3] and treachery[4] carried out over a number of years. You see, Heep falsely obtained Mr Wickfield's signature on important documents and has held him in his power ever since. First he obliged him to make him a partner. Then he systematically forged Mr Wickfield's signature on accounts and documents. Poor Mr Wickfield lost his reputation

1. **cornered:** 受困的
2. **pocket-book:** 筆記本
3. **fraud:** 詐騙
4. **treachery:** 背叛

with his clients and investors and just recently, believing himself bankrupt, signed a document giving all of the business to Heep. I have it here.'

Uriah did not speak. Agnes cried quietly, thinking of how her poor father had suffered. My aunt's reaction was quite different.

'So, you are responsible for ruining me!' she declared furiously, trying to take hold of Uriah.

'It is quite clear what must be done,' Traddles said. 'We must destroy the document giving Heep the business. Then, Heep, you must repay every penny you have stolen. If you don't, we can arrange for you to spend some time in prison.'

I still remember the look of defeat and hatred on Uriah Heep's face.

My darling Dora grew worse. She no longer left her bed and my aunt and I spent many hours sitting with her. Yet she was always so happy and loving, never complaining.

Time rolls[1] back and I can see it all so clearly. It is night and I am sitting by her bed holding her hand in mine.

---

1. rolls: 轉動

'Doady, I think I was too young and inexperienced to be a wife.'

'Don't say such things, my darling,' I say, laying my face on her pillow.

'No, Doady, it is true. We are happy now but I am sure as time goes on you will want more from your companion, more than a foolish[1] child-wife. It is better this way.'

'Oh, Dora don't!' I cry and she comforts me.

'Hush my sweet boy,' she whispers. 'Doady, I would like to talk to Agnes. Can you send her to me?' I leave reluctantly to fetch Agnes, who is downstairs with my aunt.

I sit by the fire while Agnes is with Dora. Jip, old now, is near me. My thoughts turn to Dora's words and I feel full of remorse for ever wishing her different. I sit like this for I do not know how long. Then Jip looks towards the stairs, whines[2] once and dies. Agnes comes down soon after, tears running down her face. My Dora is gone.

My grief was frozen for a time, waiting to explode fully. I do not know how but it was decided

---

1. foolish: 愚笨   2. whines: 哀鳴

that I should travel abroad for a period. Preparations were made. The time was nearing for Mr Peggotty and Emily to depart too. Mr Peggotty showed me a letter from Emily to Ham and I offered to take it to him before they left.

So, once again, I went to Yarmouth. There was a terrible storm coming. I could not find Ham and, worried, returned to the inn. Later, I was woken by voices calling out that a ship was going down so, along with others, I hurried to the beach. The broken ship was hit by wave after wave. We watched helplessly as men disappeared under the sea. Then I saw Ham and I understood his intention immediately. I tried to stop him but he pushed me aside[1] gently saying,

'If it is my time then so be it, Master Copperfield.'

With ropes around his waist[2], he went into the water. Only one man remained on the ship now, clinging to a mast. He waved his red cap in a gesture I thought familiar. Ham almost reached him but an enormous wave hit the ship then. The seamen pulled on the ropes and brought Ham

1. **aside:** 向一邊   2. **waist:** 腰部

back to shore. He was dead. Poor honest Ham! I remained with him until a fisherman asked me to follow him.

'Is there another body?' I asked. He did not reply but walked to the shore. There, lying as he used to at school, was my old friend Steerforth.

We carried his body to the inn and, in a dream-like state, I travelled to break the news to Mrs Steerforth and then directly on to London. I was determined to keep the news of Ham's death from Mr Peggotty and let them leave happy. Consequently I assured him that Ham had received the letter and his thoughts were with his uncle and Emily. Mr Peggotty boarded the ship. As he waved goodbye from the deck I saw Emily appear next to him and, placing her head on his shoulder, she waved too.

I travelled abroad from place to place, the burden[1] of my grief growing heavier and heavier. I mourned my pretty Dora, my old friend and kind-hearted Ham. At times I wanted only to die and end my sorrow[2]. Then a letter from Agnes arrived. Her gentle confidence in me gave me heart[3] and I slowly started to mend[4] and to write.

1. burden: 重擔
2. sorrow: 悲痛
3. gave (me) heart: 給我希望
4. mend: 恢復 ▶PET◀

My feelings for Agnes began to change, or rather, I understood them better. I realized I loved her and had always done so.

I returned to England three years later and went to my aunt's house in Dover. We had an emotional reunion. Talking, I asked her if Agnes had a lover. My aunt thought there was someone. I was not surprised and I resolved to hide my true feelings from Agnes, and this I did in all my visits.

It was Christmas. I had understood from my aunt that Agnes would soon marry.

'Agnes, my sister, do you not trust me with your secret?' I asked her. 'Do you think I cannot be happy for you in your marriage?' Agnes became upset and started to cry. Her look gave me hope. 'If I thought you could ever love me as more than a brother ... you must know I love you.'

'Oh, Trotwood. I have always loved you!' she said through her tears. As I held her close, I fancied[1] I saw Dora smiling at us happily, giving us her blessing[2].

We were married two weeks later.

---

1. **fancied:** 認為   2. **blessing:** 祝福

Pet Reading

1 **Look at the sentences below about the story. Decide if each sentence is correct or incorrect. If it is correct, mark A. If it is incorrect, mark B.**

1 ☐ Uriah Heep grew in height.

2 ☐ Mrs Micawber burnt the pocket-book.

3 ☐ The Micawbers were living at Mr Wickfield's house.

4 ☐ Uriah Heep wanted to take the pocket-book from Mr Micawber.

5 ☐ Mr Wickfield knew what he was doing when he signed the important documents.

6 ☐ Mr Wickfield did not want to make Heep a partner.

7 ☐ Mr Wickfield's clients were not happy.

8 ☐ Mr Wickfield was bankrupt.

9 ☐ Agnes and Aunt Betsey had the same reaction to the news.

10 ☐ Traddles decided to send Heep to prison.

Grammar

2 **Put the words in the correct order.**

1 what • It • be • is • done. • clear • quite • must

....

2 I • so • Time • it • can • all • back • clearly. • rolls • and see

....

3 will • as • on • you • am • time • I • more • goes • from companion. • want • your • sure

....

4 me • gave • confidence • Her • in • heart. • me

3 Complete the sentences with the present perfect of the verbs below and, if necessary, *for* or *since*.

be   hold   love   ~~want~~   steal

David's aunt *has wanted* to meet Mr Micawber ....*for*........ a long time.

1 Heep .... Mr Wickfield in his power .... he signed the documents.

2 Uriah Heep has to repay every penny he ....

3 Dora .... ill .... some time.

4 Agnes .... David .... she was a girl.

Vocabulary

4 Complete the table.

Noun	Adjective	Verb
....	*hateful*	....
....	*pretend*	....
....	*submissive*	....
....	*thoughtful*	....

5 Match the verbs with their definitions.

1 ☐ to tower over **a** to go onto a ship, train
2 ☐ to dismiss **b** to hold very tightly to
3 ☐ to snatch **c** to be much taller than someone
4 ☐ to cling **d** to tell someone to leave their job
5 ☐ to board **e** to take something from someone quickly

Writing

6 Write an email to a friend. Tell him or her
- What you thought of the book
- Which character you liked best/least
- Why

Charles Dickens

Charles Dickens, 1854

Childhood

Charles Dickens was born in Portsmouth in 1812. When Charles was three years old the family moved to Chatham in London. This was the happiest period of his early life. He loved reading and avidly read his father's books including *Robinson Crusoe* and *Don Quixote*. Charles could also sing and recite and he and his older sister, Fanny, were encouraged by their proud father.

Factory worker

Everything changed dramatically when his father was imprisoned for debt. The rest of the family moved into the prison too, but Charles was offered a job and sent to live with a family friend. So, aged twelve, young Charles went to work in a warehouse where he had to stick labels on shoe polish tins. He was treated quite well, but Charles found the experience humiliating. Brought up as a gentleman, he was now working with common boys. Although he only worked for a few months - a sudden inheritance released John Dickens from his debts and from prison –memories of this period and the misery he suffered remained deep and inspired much of his later writing.

Journalist

After two and a half years of school and eighteen months as an office boy, Charles, aged sixteen, declared he wanted to be a parliamentary reporter.

This was not an easy thing to do. First he had to learn shorthand, which was a long and complex job. But, inspired by his father, who had done so well, Charles devoted all his energies to it. Success was slow in coming but in 1832 he became a parliamentary reporter and a highly respected one. In fact he was considered the best and most accurate shorthand reporter there was. But it was not enough for Dickens. He wanted to write.

Cover from the original serial edition of the novel, illustrated by Phiz.

Writer

In 1834 his first original article was published and was the first of a series. Soon he was writing regularly for various periodicals. In 1836 he was asked to write a series of monthly stories about sporting life. Not knowing much about sport, he suggested an alternative and so *The Pickwick Papers* began. Dickens was just twenty-five. In 1837 *Oliver Twist* started to appear in monthly installments, followed by *Nicholas Nickleby*. Between 1836 and 1865 Dickens wrote more than twelve novels, many short stories, plays and non-fiction books. In addition to *Oliver Twist* and *Nicholas Nickleby*, the other most popular and well-known novels include *A Christmas Carol* (1843), *David Copperfield* (1849-50), and *Great Expectations* (1860-61). Many of his novels have been made into films or TV adaptations, some several times. There are at least nine film versions of *David Copperfield*.

Family

In April 1836 Charles Dickens married Catherine Hogarth. They had ten children. It was not, however, a happy marriage because they were so very different. In 1858, when their children were sufficiently grown up, they separated. Dickens died suddenly in 1870 leaving his last novel unfinished.

Life in Victorian Times

The Chimney Sweep by Jonathan Eastman Johnson 1863

Working Children

Just as, unfortunately, many children in poor countries today are forced to work, many children from poor families were obliged to work during Victorian Times. Read these questions and answers to find out more.

What age did children start work?
The age depended on the work but children as young as four were used in some factories. In mines the minimum age was five.

Where did they work?
Children worked in different places. Some worked in factories, such as textile factories, others in mines, gas works, mills, some cleaned chimneys.

How many hours did they work?
Like adults, children were made to work up to sixteen hours a day. In 1833 a Commission established the maximum number of hours children in the textile industry could work. No children under 9 could work. 11- 18 year olds could work 12 hours, 9 -11 year olds could work 8 hours. In 1842 it was extended to mines. In 1847 the working day was limited to 10 hours.

What did they do?
In factories children were often made to crawl under machinery to pick up things, clean machinery while it was running or work the machinery without talking any breaks. In mines children were sent down the smaller tunnels and pulled heavy coal carts. Little boys were also made to clean chimneys. If they got frightened their master would light a fire under them to encourage them to climb up!

What were conditions like?
Terrible! Factories were often dirty, unventilated and without natural light. Illness and disease were common as well as injury and mutilation . Pulling coal trucks in mines was awful: there was the danger of landslides, suffocation, injury, coal inhalation (the average age of death was 25). For chimney sweeps the dangers were getting stuck and suffocating, getting burnt, falls and injuries.

When did child labour stop?
A law was passed in 1870 saying that all children between 5- 10 had to attend school but children continued to work in some areas for at least another ten years.

Education

School wasn't for everyone. It was generally only for families that could afford it, although there were Sunday Schools organized by the Church and day schools organized by charities for poorer children. Despite this in 1840 only about 20% of children went to school. Children from rich families had nannies and governesses to teach them then, when they were old enough, the boys were sent away to school. Girls normally stayed at home and learnt how to sing, play the piano and other accomplishments suitable for young ladies. During the Victorian Age many new schools were set up and it seems that anyone could do it! David Copperfield's experience at Salem House was a sad reality

for many boys while any room was good enough to use as a classroom. After 1870, education became compulsory.

But they didn't learn all the subjects we learn today. Most only learnt to read, write and do arithmetic.

A Stagecoach Setting Out
by John Charles Maggs 1873

Travel

How did people travel around the country before there were cars, buses and trains? They used a stagecoach. These were four-wheeled vehicles pulled by horses that travelled regularly between towns. Like buses and coaches today, they ran to a timetable. There were seats inside the coach and up on top, behind or next to the driver. These were not so good if the weather was bad! Stagecoaches followed a specific route and stopped on the way at 'stages', a bit like buses stop at bus stops today. The stages were at inns (a type of hotel) where passengers could rest and eat before continuing their journey. David Copperfield travelled to London by stagecoach when he went to school.

Decide if the following statements about education are true (T) or false (F).

T F

1 Families with a law income sent their children to Sunday Schools.

2 Only qualified teachers could open new schools during the Victorian Age.

3 Up until 1870 children didn't have to go to school by law.

Test yourself 自測

Complete the crossword.

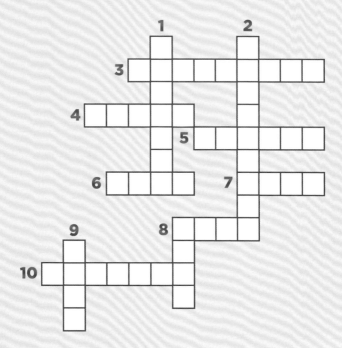

Across

3 Where David worked as a child. (9 letters)
4 If your bread is like this, don't throw it out. You can feed it to the ducks. (5 letters)
5 Aunt Betsey wore one. (six letters)
6 Some dogs do this too much. (4 letters)
7 Give a big smile. (4 letters)
8 Mr. Barkis drove one. (4 letters)
10 Uriah Heep was one. (7 letters)

Down

1 People sat in this room in the past. (7 letters)
2 Another way of saying two weeks. (9 letters)
8 Children were punished with this. (4 letters)
9 It's a good idea to write one in case of death. (4 letters)

Syllabus 語法重點和學習主題

//

Topics
Clothes, daily life, work, family, home, emotions, people

Tenses
Present simple: states, habits
Past simple: finished time
Past continuous: actions in progress at a specific time in past, interrupted actions
Present perfect simple: indefinite past, unfinished past
Past perfect: narrative
Futures: will/shall, present continuous

Verb forms
Imperatives
Passives: present, past simple
Gerunds: after verbs, prepositions

Conditionals:
1st conditional: possible present/future
2nd conditional: hypothetical present/future

Reported speech:
statements, questions, commands

Modals
Can, could: ability, permission
May, might: possibility, permission
Must, have to: obligation
Defining, non-defining clauses,
Purpose clauses
Linkers
So + adjective, such (a) + adjective + noun

Answer Key 答案

David Copperfield

Pages 6-7
1 **1** i **2** d **3** g **4** c **5** e **6** b **7** h **8** a
3 **1** as **2** a **3** to **4** the **5** a **6** at **7** old **8** his **9** nurse **10** back **11** tells **12** up
4 **a** severe **b** calm **c** arrogant **d** formidable **e** kind-hearted

Pages 16-17
1 **1** F **2** T **3** T **4** T **5** F **6** T **7** F
2 **1** disapprovingly **2** inconsolable **3** displease **4** uneasy
3 suggested answers

Physical features/body	Personality
whiskers eyes	loving affectionate indulgent
shoulders curls nose	stern nervous anxious
eyebrows hand	disobedient

4 **1** didn't use to **2** used to **3** didn't use to **4** used to **5** used to
6 **1** House **2** square/brick **3** 0/none **4** desks **5** careful

Pages 26-27
1 **1** A **2** C **3** A **4** B **5** D **6** C **7** C **8** B **9** A **10** D
2 **1** was waiting, arrived **2** returned, found **3** was sitting, entered **4** got, saw **5** were, dined
6 was having, went
3 **1** F **2** T **3** T **4** T

Pages 36-37
1 **1** He thought his presence might irritate Mr Murdstone's conscience.
2 It was situated on the waterfront in Blackfriars.
3 David earned six shillings a week.
4 Mr Micawber had financial problems.
2 **1** sent it abroad by ship **2** accommodation was **3** total humiliation **4** asked for my help
5 started crying
3 **1** There were **2** to pay **3** was arrested **4** if he remembered **5** as kind as
4 **1** F **2** T **3** T **4** F **5** T

Pages 46-47
1 **A** 7 **B** 6 **C** 4 **D** 2 **E** 8 **F** 1 **G** 3 **H** 9 **I** 5
2 **1** c **2** a **3** f **4** e **5** d **6** b
3 **1** grew **2** knew **3** saw **4** spent, taught **5** found **6** fell
5 **1** b **2** d **3** a **4** e **5** c

Pages 56-57
1 **1** Who did David and Dora tell about their engagement?
2 What tested David and Dora's love?
3 Why was Dora sent to live with two old aunts?
4 How did Mr Wickfield react when he realized Uriah Heep wanted to marry Agnes?
5 How old was David when he got married?
6 Why did Mr Peggotty decide to emigrate to Australia?
2 **1** wouldn't watch, didn't consider
2 will change, give up
3 weren't, wouldn't need
4 think, will forgive

3 model answer

Dear Mary,

Thank you so much for your letter. You asked about our wedding and married life. Well, the wedding was a simple quiet affair. There were only David, myself and our aunts present but I wore a pretty dress and David gave me some lovely flowers. Married life is wonderful! I am so happy! We have a little house in Highgate. David works hard and often writes in the evenings too. I sit by him with a supply of pens ready for him to use. I must confess I am not good at cooking or accounts so it is really the only thing I can do to help.

Write to me soon

Best wishes

Dora

4 **1** such a **2** so **3** such **4** so

5 **1** He received a letter.

2 He wanted to meet David and Traddles.

3 Mr Micawber was agitated.

4 He wanted to introduce Mr Micawber to his aunt.

5 He wanted them to go to Canterbury.

Pages 68-69

1 **1** B **2** B **3** B **4** A **5** B **6** A **7** A **8** B **9** B **10** B

2 **1** It is quite clear what must be done.

2 Time rolls back and I can see it all so clearly.

3 I am sure as time goes on you will want more from your companion.

4 Her confidence in me gave me heart.

3 **1** has held, since **2** has stolen **3** has been, for **4** has loved, since

4

Noun	Adjective	Verb
hate	hateful	*hate*
pretence	pretend	*pretend*
submission	submissive	*submit*
thought	thoughtful	*think*

5 **1** c **2** d **3** e **4** b **5** a

6 model answer

Hi Sam,

I've just read *David Copperfield* and really enjoyed it. I'm not really sure who I liked best in the book but I know who I liked least: Mr Murdstone. He was very cruel and made David very unhappy. Try reading it, I'm sure you'll like it!

Bye for now

Jemma

Page 76

Read for Pleasure: *David Copperfield* 塊肉餘生

作　　者：Charles Dickens
改　　寫：Alex Peet
繪　　畫：Felicita Sala
照　　片：Corbis, Eli Archives
責任編輯：黃家麗
封面設計：涂　慧
出　　版：商務印書館（香港）有限公司
　　　　　香港筲箕灣耀興道 3 號東滙廣場 8 樓
　　　　　http://www.commercialpress.com.hk
發　　行：香港聯合書刊物流有限公司
　　　　　香港新界荃灣德士古道 220-248 號荃灣工業中心 16 樓
印　　刷：中華商務彩色印刷有限公司
　　　　　香港新界大埔汀麗路 36 號中華商務印刷大廈 14 字樓
版　　次：2022 年 6 月第 1 版第 2 次印刷
　　　　　© 2016 商務印書館（香港）有限公司
　　　　　ISBN 978 962 07 0463 5
　　　　　Printed in Hong Kong
　　　　　版權所有　不得翻印

Read for Pleasure 系列為高小至初中英語學習者提供英文讀本,包括經典名著和現代故事,分Basic、Intermediate 和 Advanced 三級。內容豐富,設計具現代感,在享受閱讀之樂的同時,可提升聽說讀寫的能力。

大衛原與母親相依為命,繼父的出現給他的生活帶來翻天覆地的改變,家裏經常彌漫着惶恐不安。大衛先後被送入寄宿學校和工廠,吃盡苦頭,而對他最大的打擊,莫過於慈母離世,今後他將何去何從呢?

查爾斯‧狄更斯筆鋒銳利,作品描繪光怪陸離的社會現象,代表作有《苦海孤雛》、《雙城記》、《塊肉餘生》等。

掃描 **QR code** 聆聽故事錄音

Level	Number of Headwords	Cambridge Examinations
Basic	600 – 800 headwords	Movers Flyers/Key (KET)
Intermediate	1000 – 1600 headwords	Preliminary (PET)
Advanced	1800 – 2500 headwords	First (FCE) Advanced

文化閱讀 購物平台
mybookone.com.hk

ISBN 978 962 07 0463 5
HK$ 65.00

9 789620 704635

陳列類別:英語學習

代理商 聯合出版
電話 02-25868596
NT: 290.

聯合出版集團

商務印書館(香港)有限公司
THE COMMERCIAL PRESS (HK) LTD.

William Shakespeare

Much Ado About Nothing

無 事 生 非

商務印書館

Level 5